Supermarket Zoo

For Tinka and Puppy **xxx** – C.H.
For Becs **x** – E.E.

SIMON AND SCHUSTER
First published in Great Britain in 2010 by Simon and Schuster UK Ltd
1st Floor, 222 Gray's Inn Road, London WC1X 8HB
A CBS Company

Text copyright © 2010 Caryl Hart
Illustrations copyright © 2010 Edward Eaves

A CIP catalogue record for this book is available from the British Library upon request

ISBN: 978-1-84738-477-5 (HB)
ISBN: 978-1-4711-4346-5 (PB)

Printed in China
10 9 8 7 6

Supermarket Zoo

Caryl Hart & Ed Eaves

SIMON AND SCHUSTER
London   New York   Sydney

The minute I wake up, I know something is different, but I can't quite figure out what.

It's probably nothing.

So I pick up my ball
and I am just going
out to play when . . .

"Albie!"

It's Mum. She has her car keys in one hand and a pile of bags in the other. This can only mean one thing – **shopping!**

DISASTER!

I HATE shopping!

But Mum has me trapped and there's nothing I can do.

At the supermarket, the first thing
I notice is our trolley. It's **enormous** —
I can't even reach the handle.
And there's a really **funny** smell.

Mum doesn't seem to notice, she just hands me the shopping list and sets off.

6 monkeys

2 giraffes

Fresh lizards

3 kilos tortoises

27 parrots (give or take)

Pride of lions

2 bales of hay

5 tins of lion food

Vegetables, fruit, nuts

Tyr● ●·· ·

"Right," says Mum. "Reptiles first.
Chameleons or iguanas? We'll need two."

This is **mad!**
But Mum seems to think it's completely normal.

I pick out two green-and-orange chameleons and place them in the trolley. Mum says, "Gently now, don't bruise them!"

We hurry past the rattlesnakes and cobras, to the tortoises. I spot a sign saying:

FREE SALAD WITH EVERY TORTOISE.

So we take three.

Next we pass the cool cabinets. I say, "Can we get a penguin?" Mum sighs, "OK, but get one from the back because it'll be fresher."

Then this polar bear smiles at me.
"Pleeeease,"
I say.
But Mum is cross.
"No, not today."

At the giraffes, we pick a
Mother-and-Baby Special.

Then we head off to find some parrots.

I've never heard such **screeching** and **squawking**.
I like the toucans best but Mum says, "It's parrots
or nothing."

People say it's good luck if a bird poops
on your head, but I don't think Mum agrees!

Next on the list are the monkeys.
Now everyone knows monkeys are tricky,
but have you ever tried getting six of them
to sit in a trolley full of pecking parrots?
It's **impossible!**

In the end, I have to open a packet
of nuts to keep them all quiet.

Then we get to the lions.
Now, I love watching big cats on TV, but to look straight into
the wide eyes of a hungry lion, **well that's something else!**

Mum chooses one of the meanest looking beasts I've ever seen. "I'll go and find the lion food," I say. Not that I'm scared or anything.

We pile in bags of carrots, monkey nuts, bananas, seeds and mangoes. By the time we get to the check-out the trolley is so **heavy** I can hardly push it.

Mum heaves our shopping onto the conveyor belt while I start to pack.

It's a **big** job.

We are nearly done when Mum rushes off shouting, "Keep going, I won't be a minute!" She always forgets **something** . . .

But I wasn't expecting this!

Outside, we open the car. It looks so small.
It's lucky that mums are so good at packing
or we'd have never got everything in.

Well, I told you this morning that I thought something was different — and it turns out I was right! This has been the best shopping trip ever. Just look at all my new friends! **I wonder what we'll buy next week . . .**

Things to buy from the Monster Market:

2 spotted furzelwurzels

3 bouncing bongle tweezles

3 kilos of bug-eyed flomstrops

Warp garglers

Blimps

Noozles or bog-tromplers